FLOWER GARDEN

WRITTEN BY

Eve Bunting

ILLUSTRATED BY

Kathryn Hewitt

VOYAGER BOOKS

HARCOURT, INC.

Orlando Austin New York San Diego Toronto London

www.HarcourtBooks.com

First Voyager Books edition 2000
Voyager Books is a registered trademark of Harcourt, Inc.

The Library of Congress has catalogued the hardcover edition as follows:
Bunting, Eve.
Flower garden/Eve Bunting; illustrated by Kathryn Hewitt
p. cm.
Summary: Helped by her father, a young girl prepares
a flower garden as a birthday surprise for her mother.
(1. Gardening — Fiction. 2. Parent and child — Fiction. 3. Birthdays — Fiction.
4. Stories in rhyme.) I. Hewitt, Kathryn, ill. II. Title.
PZ8.3.B92F1 1994
(E) — dc20 92-25766
ISBN-13: 978-0-15-228776-0 ISBN-10: 0-15-228776-0
ISBN-13: 978-0-15-202372-0 pb ISBN-10: 0-15-202372-0 pb

S T

Printed in Singapore

The paintings in this book were done in oil paint on paper
The display type and text type were set in Benguiat
Color separations by Bright Arts, Ltd., Singapore
Printed and bound by Tien Wah Press, Singapore
Production supervision by Stanley Redfern and Pascha Gerlinger
Designed by Lisa Peters

Garden on the checkout stand
I can hardly wait.

Garden in a cardboard box
Walking to the bus

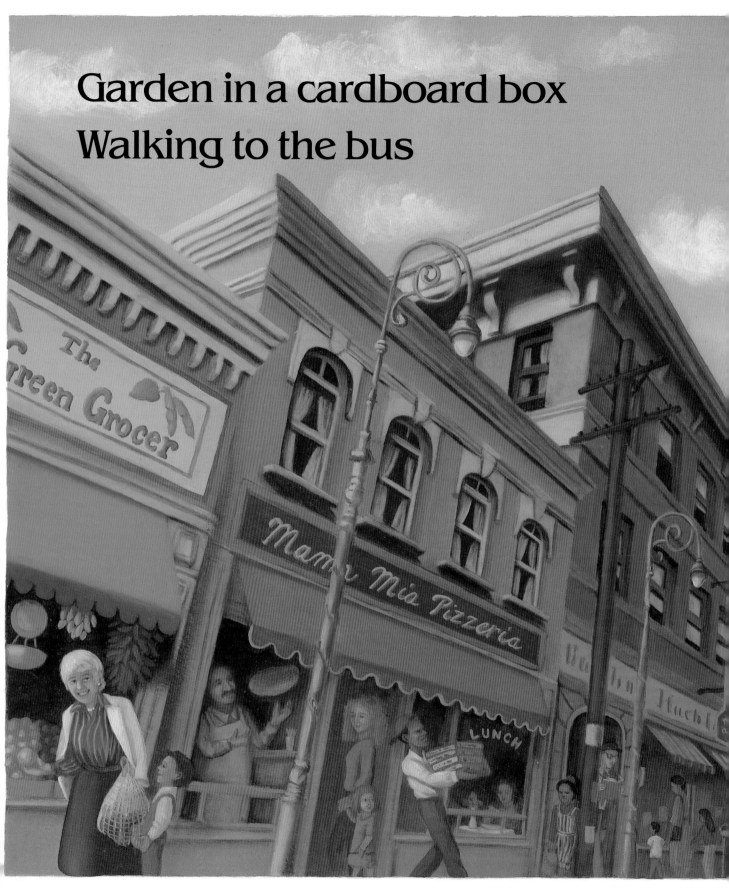

Garden sitting on our laps
People smile at us!

Garden going up the stairs
Stopping at each floor

This garden's getting heavier!
At last — our own front door.

Hurry! Hurry! Get the trowel
Spread the papers thick.

Get the bag of potting soil
Get the planting mix.

Daffodils, geraniums and tulips in a row.

Garden in a window box
High above the street

Where butterflies
can stop and rest
And ladybugs can meet.

Walkers walking down below
Will lift their heads and see
Purple, yellow, red, and white
A color jamboree.

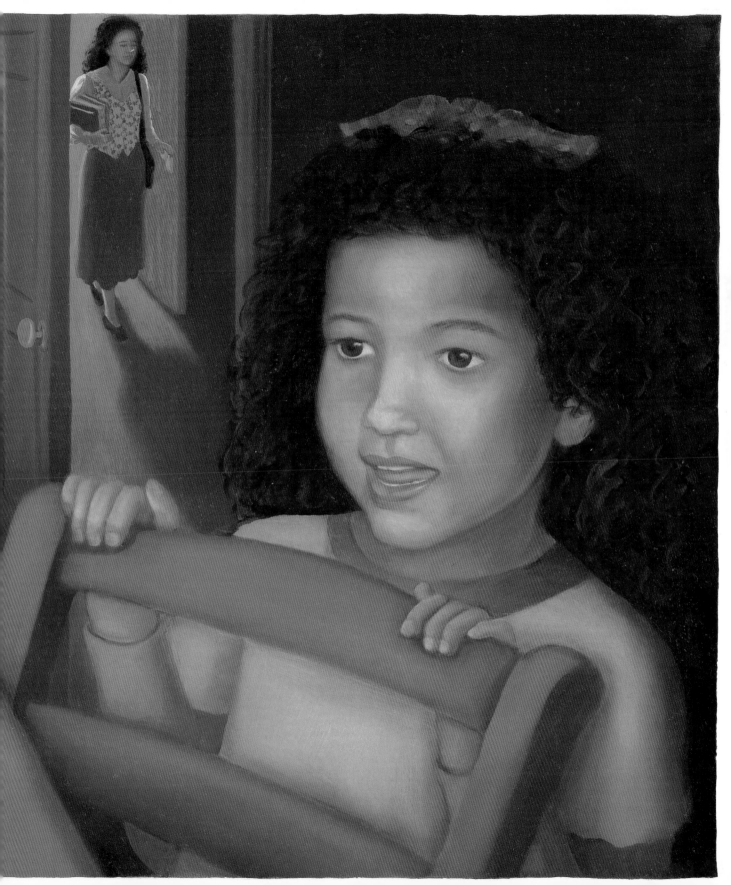

Happy, happy birthday, Mom!
A garden box — for you.